# In the Sky at Nighttime

Published by Inhabit Media Inc.
www.inhabitmedia.com

Inhabit Media Inc. (Iqaluit) P.O. Box 11125, Iqaluit, Nunavut, X0A 1H0
(Toronto) 191 Eglinton Avenue East, Suite 310, Toronto, Ontario, M4P 1K1

Design and layout copyright © 2019 Inhabit Media Inc.
Text copyright © 2019 Laura Deal
Illustrations by Tamara Campeau © 2019 Inhabit Media Inc.

Editors: Neil Christopher and Kelly Ward
Art director: Danny Christopher

This project was made possible in part by the Government of Canada.

We acknowledge the support of the Canada Council for the Arts for our publishing program.

Printed in Canada

# In the Sky at Nighttime

by Laura Deal

illustrated by Tamara Campeau

INHABIT
MEDIA

In the sky at nighttime,
our laughter twists through the crisp, cold air.

2

We watch the northern lights dance and twirl,
painting bright colours across the endless sky.

In the sky at nighttime,
the stars flicker on the clearest of nights.

8

Silently, a hunter returns from the land,
a single speck of light crossing the bay.

In the sky at nighttime,
snow falls fast.

10

The glowing full moon illuminates the ground
as the snow crunches beneath our feet.

In the sky at nighttime,
a raven roosts atop a tall building.

Calling out through the dark,
he tells others of his find.

17

In the sky at nighttime,
a mother's delicate song to her child rises
like a gentle breeze.

They rock together, swaying in rhythm.

In the sky at nighttime,
the dreams of many, magical and extraordinary,
swirl as we rest.

At peace with the day ahead
and the one we leave behind.

25

Laura Deal lives in Iqaluit, Nunavut, and is originally from Musquodoboit, Nova Scotia. She enjoys writing and many other forms of creative arts. She believes it is important for children, like her daughter, to see their own stories reflected in the pages of Northern-based storybooks. Laura is the author of *How Nivi Got Her Names*, which is also available as a short film.

Tamara Campeau is an illustrator residing in a small town called Port-Cartier in northern Quebec. She studied at Sheridan College, where she spent four years attaining her bachelor of illustration. When she is not illustrating, she can be found working out outside or at the local gym, or spending time with her better half and their brown poodle, Pinut.

Inhabit Media Inc.
Iqaluit • Toronto